2

Animals Galore

•

Diane Redmond

2

Animals Galore

•

Diane Redmond

MACDONALD YOUNG BOOKS

For my daughter, Isabella, and all her animals

With endless thanks to
Simon Gower, BVSc, MRCVS.

– D.R.

Text copyright © Diane Redmond 1998

First published in Great Britain in 1998
by Macdonald Young Books
an imprint of Wayland Publishers Ltd
61 Western Road
Hove
East Sussex
BN3 1JD

Printed and bound in Guernsey
by The Guernsey Press Co. Ltd

ISBN: 0 7500 2418 6

The Animal
SANCTUARY

1
New Friends

2
Animals Galore

3
Animal Alert

4
Animals at Home

1

When Jess woke up on the first day of the new spring term there was an unusual stillness hanging in the air. From downstairs she could hear the insistent miaowing of Puss and Boots the kittens, fussing for their breakfast, but outside all was eerily quiet. Puzzled Jess walked across to the window and threw open her curtains. The scene that met her eyes was breathtaking.

"*Snow!*" she gasped as she gazed across the Sanctuary gardens to the rolling Lancashire moors where the high tops sparkled with the first fall of the year. "*Wake up!*" she called out to her sleeping brothers and sister. Daisy and Danny, the nine-year-old twins, came tearing into her room, their eyes bright and round as blue saucers with excitement.

"Snowballs!" they yelled as they pushed open Jess's window and started to scoop up handfuls of snow.

Luke, the eldest, came shuffling in, bleary-eyed and yawning. Two snowballs landing on his head and chest woke him up with an icy shock.

"Right! I'll get you," he laughed.

Still in their pyjamas, they all tore downstairs to the hall, where they briefly stopped to grab their wellies and anoraks, then raced out into the garden. Wild with excitement, Poppy and Digger, the family's black Labradors, chased after them trying to catch the whizzing snowballs. Twice the dogs disappeared from sight as they dived headlong into snowdrifts and came up barking, covered in snow. Puss and Boots came scampering out through the cat-flap to see what the fuss was about. As their dainty feet hit the ice-cold they stopped dead in their tracks and miaowed forlornly.

"Don't be wimps," said Daisy as she bent down to kiss their pretty little heads. "This is fun!"

Puss and Boots gave her a disdainful look then scampered back into the kitchen where they curled up in their basket by the old Aga cooker.

"Let's make a snowman," cried Danny.

Just as they started rolling a huge ball to make the snowman, Nutty the donkey brayed from across the yard.

"EE-AAAW!"

"Poor old thing, he's waiting for his breakfast," said Jess, running off towards his stable.

"Wait for me," Danny called after her.

When Nutty heard the sound of their approaching feet on the path he hung his head over the stable door and brayed even louder.

"OK, Nuts. We haven't forgotten you," soothed Jess as she fastened a head collar around the donkey and opened the stable door to lead him out into the paddock. "Come on, let's make footprints in the snow."

Nutty lifted his head and huffed and puffed excitedly, sending up flumes of steam as his warm breath hit the sharp, frosty air. When Danny appeared with his feed the greedy donkey ducked his head into the bucket and munched contentedly on his favourite pony nuts.

"Do you think he'll be warm enough in this weather?" Jess fretted.

"Of course," laughed Danny, rubbing his hand through the donkey's warm fur. "Just look how thick his coat is."

Nutty finished his feed then licked Jess's dark curly hair, as if to say, is there any more? Jess giggled and tickled his long ears.

"That's your lot," she said firmly. "At least until we get back from school."

"If the weather's this bad maybe there won't be any school," said Danny hopefully.

"Dream on!" laughed Jess.

Dad had cleared a path down the drive.

"To let the customers in and you lot out!" he teased as they set off for school.

10

"We might be back if the school bus doesn't turn up," Jess warned.

"Good," laughed Beryl the veterinary nurse. "I could *do* with an extra pair of hands to clean out the dog run and hose down the yard!"

Still throwing snowballs at each other they ran across Moorside village green where the twins went one way to their primary school and the older two headed for the bus stop. Waiting for them were their best friends, Beth and Sam Mars.

"Nice weather," said Luke shoving a handful of snow down Sam's back.

Sam grimaced as the snow slipped over his shoulders.

"For penguins!" he said as he bent to roll a snowball and stuff it up Luke's jumper.

"Watch out," Beth warned. "Here comes the bus."

They all jumped backwards as the school bus came to a slow halt, sending out a spray of muddy brown slush. Once on the packed bus, the girls dashed to sit in their favourite seats at the front.

"I've had a brilliant idea," announced Beth.

Jess absently wiped the steamy bus window and peered out at Moorside village, pretty as a picture postcard beneath its soft quilt of white snow.

"Listen, Jess," Beth urged. "I want to raise money for the donkey sanctuary in Saddleworth."

Jess instantly switched her attention from the view to Beth.

"What gave you that idea?"

"Their newsletter. They desperately need money for more grazing land and a new stable block." Beth's large, hazel eyes were serious. "Honestly, Jess, when I looked at the pictures of all those abandoned donkeys I felt I *had* to do something."

"Right," said Jess, who was just as tender-hearted about animals as Beth. "How are you going to raise the money?"

"I'm going to organize a pet competition at school and ask Mr Warburton to judge it," Beth announced with a triumphant smile.

Jess giggled. Mr Warburton was the head of the first year and a bit of a scientific boffin. He had untidy hair, a grey beard that was usually full of biscuit crumbs and half-moon glasses that he peered over in a vague sort of way.

"Is Mr Warburton your best bet?" joked Jess. "I mean, he's so absent-minded he wouldn't even notice if there was a rabbit standing in front of him eating a lettuce!"

Beth didn't smile at the joke but stared ahead with an anxious expression on her face.

"Actually, the animals are worrying me," she blurted out.

"You can't have an animal competition without *animals*," laughed Jess.

"I know," Beth replied in an exasperated voice. "I'm just thinking of the organization. The dogs will fight, the cats will run away and how can we take large animals into school?"

"We could have a competition for small pets," Jess suggested. "You know, mice and hamsters and gerbils."

Beth shook her head, not convinced.

"It's a bit *babyish*."

They both stared thoughtfully out of the window and watched the quiet country lanes give way to the busy main roads leading into Manchester.

As the bus conductor approached to check their tickets Jess suddenly cried out, "Rabbits!"

The conductor burst out laughing and said,

"We don't go there, will Manchester do?"

Blushing Jess handed over her pass and waited for the conductor to move further up the bus.

"Rabbits?" she repeated excitedly.

Beth looked blank.

"What about them?"

"Think about it," Jess urged. "At least six people have got rabbits in our class. There are four year groups and if there are five or six people in each class with a rabbit we'd have at least twenty for the show. And they'd be in cages which makes the organization much easier."

Beth nodded excitedly.

"Brilliant," she said. "Let's check out the numbers in the other first year classes then we'll make a decision."

At playtime Beth and Jess carried out their market research. After quarter of an hour's investigation they had a clear answer.

"Twenty rabbits," exclaimed Beth.

"Twenty-one with Danny's rabbit," Jess added.

"Will he let you bring Pepsi into school?" Beth enquired.

"He might be persuaded," Jess answered with a knowing wink.

Beth consulted a row of figures in her maths exercise book.

"If we charge fifty pence for every entry and get twenty-one rabbits I could make ten pounds fifty pence," she announced. "Now all I've got to do is get Mr Warburton's permission to have the competition in school."

"Don't forget to ask him to judge it too," Jess reminded her.

When Jess and Luke got home from school Mum, Dad and Beryl were in the farmyard behind the Sanctuary eagerly watching a huge articulated truck being unloaded.

"Hi, there!" called mum as Jess and Luke ran to join them. "The roof timbers for the large animal hospital have just arrived."

"It won't be long now to the opening at Easter," said Beryl excitedly.

"Oh, it can't come quick enough for me," sighed Mum.

Jess's mind flashed back six months, to the days when they'd lived in London and Mum and Dad had run a thriving veterinary practice in a busy suburb. Then out of the blue they'd announced their plan to move north and open a large animal hospital. The children had all gone ballistic! They'd hated the idea of moving to Manchester, two hundred miles away from their friends and relatives. But Mum had always dreamed of opening her own large animal hospital and Moorside Sanctuary, with all its land and outbuildings, had furnished that dream. The animal hospital, growing daily before their very eyes, was Mrs Church's pride and joy.

"Only a couple of months now," Jess whispered.

Mum nodded and smiled.

"I know, Jess. I'm counting the days."

Not only had Mum's dreams come true with the move north but the rest of the family were happy too. Now, after six wonderful months of living in Moorside, Jess couldn't even think of moving back to

London. The Sanctuary was her home and she loved everything about it. The house, the moors, the village, her school and her new friends. Her thoughts were suddenly interrupted by the twins, noisily rushing across the yard.

"Wowee!" yelled Danny as he gazed at the huge roof timbers dangling from a crane. "They're big."

"Everything's big in Mum's large animal hospital!" laughed Dad.

2

Mr Warburton gave his permission for Beth to hold her competition and the following week twenty-one rabbits, including Pepsi, were brought into school. There were dwarf rabbits and lop-eared, Dutch, English, Californian, Himalayan and rare breeds like an Angora and Chinchilla.

"Mr Warburton's going to have a job judging this lot," said Luke as he inspected the rabbits. "There are some real beauties.

Look at that amazing Angora. Its fur must be at least eight centimetres long."

"I prefer the little Dutch rabbits," said Beth as she stroked the silky ears of a baby chocolate brown rabbit.

"None of them are as pretty as Danny's Pepsi," said Luke loyally.

"What do you think, Jess?" He looked across at his sister who was staring intently into the one of the rabbits' cages. "Jess!" he called sharply.

Jess turned to him, her brow creased with anxiety.

"There's something wrong with this rabbit," she said.

The others quickly crossed to where she was standing and peered at the pure white Albino rabbit with pink eyes, crouched in the corner of his cage.

"That's Buttons," said Beth. "He belongs to Alex in our class."

"He looks really sick," said Luke. "He's drooling and look at the thick white stuff coming out of his eyes and nose."

Jess stared hard at her brother.

"He reminds me of the rabbit that came to Dad's surgery in London," she said. "Do you remember?"

"Yes. The black one that nearly died," Luke replied. "It had snuffles."

"What's snuffles?" Beth demanded impatiently.

"It's a *really* dangerous bacterial bug," Jess told her.

Beth went pale with shock.

"You mean Buttons could die?" she gasped.

"I hope not," Jess replied. "But I think he needs attention."

"What about all the other rabbits?" Sam asked, staring around the hall at the cages on the tables. "They could *all* be at risk!"

"Oh, no..." muttered Beth.

"If it's that bad we should cancel the contest," said Sam firmly.

"How can we? All the rabbits are here now," Jess pointed out.

"Alex should never have brought Buttons into school," fumed Beth.

"She probably doesn't even realize," Luke reasoned. "Anyway we could be wrong."

"Oh..." sighed Jess. "I do *hope* we're wrong."

The pleasure of watching Mr Warburton judge the competition was completely ruined for Jess. As he slowly and very methodically examined every single rabbit, Jess had only one thought going round and round inside her head.

"Be quick! Please, be quick!"

Pepsi, who was in his cage right next door to Buttons hopped about excitedly when Mr Warburton approached him.

"Well at least Pepsi's lively," whispered Beth, trying to think of something positive to cheer Jess up.

"For the moment," muttered Jess gloomily.

When Mr Warburton lifted Buttons out of his cage he took one look at him then quickly put him back.

"Goodness, is your rabbit all right, Alex?" he asked his owner.

"He's only got a bit of a cold," said Alex, blushing furiously.

"*Only!*" whispered Jess to Luke. "She's got to be joking!"

An hour later Mr Warburton came to his decision and awarded the Angora rabbit the first prize. Even the ten pounds fifty pence Beth had raised for the donkey sanctuary, plus the extra five pounds that Mr Warburton had generously donated, didn't bring a smile to Jess's face.

"I just wish Alex would get her rabbit out of here," she whispered to Beth as she moved Pepsi's cage as far way from Buttons as possible.

It was a huge relief to get back home. Even though it was a bit gloomy and overcast Jess hurried out into the garden where she put Pepsi in his rabbit run.

"The fresh air will do you good," she told him.

When Danny saw his rabbit, he rushed across the lawn shouting,

"Did he win?"

"No. Mr Warburton chose an Angora," Jess told him.

Danny's cheerful smile fell away.

"Oh..." he said in a disappointed voice.

"But I thought he was the best and so did Luke," Jess assured him. "I've given him a carrot as a treat and I'll buy you an ice-cream on Saturday, when I get my pocket money."

Danny instantly cheered up.

"You really are the best," he told Pepsi as he bent to gently stroke his rabbit's silky ear. "A star!"

Jess gulped hard and tried not to think about the sick rabbit that Pepsi had spent the whole day with.

When Mr Church came out of his consulting room later on that evening he found Jess sitting at his desk, surrounded by veterinary manuals.

"What're you reading?" he asked curiously.

"I'm trying to find out about snuffles," she told him.

"Why?"

"I think one of the rabbits in the school pet competition has it," she said.

"*What*!" gasped Mr Church.

Jess nodded.

"Describe the symptoms to me," he said, quickly sitting down beside her.

"Thick, white discharge from the eyes and nose, constant drooling, dull and sleepy."

24

"Oh, dear," he sighed. "They're the classic symptoms."

Jess nodded.

"The piece I've been reading in here," said Jess, tapping a veterinary journal, "says it's highly contagious and can be a killer."

"It can be, unless it's diagnosed early and intensively treated with antibiotics," Dad told her.

Jess closed the heavy book and sighed heavily.

"Beth and I organized that competition, Dad. It's our fault that all those rabbits have been exposed to snuffles and it'll be our fault if they die," she added close to tears.

"Nonsense," her father replied briskly. "Probably none of them will die. But they ought to be checked over," he added quickly.

"How can we be sure they'll all be seen by a vet?" Jess cried. Suddenly her face lit up. "Dad!" she exclaimed. "You could do it."

"Me?" he laughed. "That's impossible! I can't travel all around Manchester examining rabbits that might have snuffles."

"You wouldn't have to travel anywhere if they all came into school," Jess said.

Dad stared at her curiously.

"If I can organize an after-school clinic you could personally check over every single rabbit," she said.

"Thanks, Jess," Dad chuckled. "As if I haven't got enough to do already."

3

The next day Jess talked to Mr Warburton and got permission to hold an after school rabbit clinic on Friday afternoon.

"We've got to make sure that every single rabbit comes back for a check-up," she told Beth. "It's vital that we don't leave anybody out."

"What about Alex?" Beth asked. "No way do we want her turning up with Buttons."

"Dad's phoning her parents this morning,"

Jess told her.

"But what do we say to Alex when we see her?" Beth fretted.

"We'll worry about that when we see her," Jess replied firmly.

It turned out that Alex wasn't in school that day anyway.

"Is she ill?" Jess asked her best friend.

"No, she was too upset to come in this morning," her friend explained. "Her rabbit died last night and Alex is really gutted."

A look of alarm flashed between Jess and Beth.

"Blimey!" Jess murmured. "This thing could get seriously out of hand."

That afternoon, as soon as Jess got home, she dashed across the lawn to see Pepsi in his rabbit run. He was quietly nibbling the grass but Jess immediately imagined twenty different things wrong with him. Luke found her staring at the rabbit like a hawk stares at a field mouse.

"Do you think he looks all right?" she murmured as her brother approached.

Luke knelt down beside her and stared at Pepsi.

"He's a bit quiet," he said thoughtfully.

It was all Jess needed.

"Oh, no!" she cried. "Do you think he's got snuffles? What will Danny do if he dies? It's all my fault for taking Pepsi into school in the first place."

"Jess, cool it!" laughed Luke. "I only said he looked quiet. I didn't say he looked as if he had a killer bug, for crying out loud."

Jess smiled, rather self-consciously.

"I'm so worried," she muttered.

"Get Mum or Dad to give him the once over," Luke suggested.

"I will, when they've finished their evening surgeries," she replied.

Seeing her anxious expression Luke said, "Come and give Bonny her tea. That's always good for a laugh."

Bonny, the family's pet cockatoo, was perching moodily in her large cage in the sitting room. At the sight of visitors she instantly cheered up and hopped excitedly on her bars.

"Fancy a cuppa?" she cackled loudly.

"Not right now, thanks," chatted Luke. "I was thinking of letting you have a fly around while I cleaned out your cage."

Bonny cocked her head as if she were thinking over his suggestion then burst out cackling.

"Give us a kiss!"

"Mad as a hatter, you are," laughed Luke as he opened the cage door. "Let's see you shake a tail feather," he added, holding out his hand for the bird to hop on to.

Bonny blinked snootily then graciously stepped on to his extended hand.

"Who's a lovely boy then?" she crooned as she rubbed her head up and down against his cheek.

Jess burst into a fit of giggles.

"She's about the only female in the world who fancies you!" she teased.

Luke gently stroked Bonny's fine feathers.

"She's about the only female in the world with good taste," he answered back.

Bonny gave Luke's ear a tender nibble then she flew off around the room shrieking with pleasure.

After Bonny had been cleaned and fed Jess went in search of Mrs Church who was just winding up her evening surgery.

She waited patiently for a very old spaniel with weepy eyes and a slow, stately walk to leave the room then dashed in.

"I'm really worried about Pepsi," she blurted out.

"Don't be," Mum said cheerfully. "He's in fine health.'

"How do you know?"

"I examined him this morning. He's fine," Mum assured her. "Though I must remember to trim his toenails."

"Alex's rabbit died yesterday," Jess said.

"I know," Mum replied. "Dad talked to the family this morning."

"Was it snuffles?"

"Sounds like it to me," Mum replied.

"Thank goodness Dad's doing the rabbit clinic on Friday."

Mum nodded in agreement.

"The sooner the better."

Every single person who'd entered the competition brought their rabbit back to school. As they gathered in the hall there was a very tense atmosphere. Dad did his best to try and calm everybody down but some of the owners were beginning to panic. One girl burst into tears.

"I don't want my rabbit to die like Buttons did," she sobbed.

"I don't think any of your rabbits will die," Dad soothed. "I just want to give them a thorough examination then you can all go home feeling more relaxed."

One by one the pupils queued up with their pets to see Mr Church who gently and very thoroughly examined all of the rabbits. He paid particular attention to the insides of their mouths, runny eyes, and listened intently to their chests to check their breathing was clear. Jess's heart lurched in fear when a boy stood at the front of the queue holding a rabbit with streaming eyes and a slobbery mouth.

"Oh, no! Not another one," she muttered under her breath to Beth.

Mr Church didn't bat an eyelid. Instead he calmly opened the rabbit's mouth and shone a small bright light inside. The rabbit wriggled uncomfortably as Dad carefully examined its teeth and gums.

"I'm afraid your rabbit has got rotten, overgrown teeth and inflamed gums," he told the rabbit's owner.

Instead of looking upset the boy smiled with relief.

"Thank goodness it's not that killer bug!" he exclaimed.

"No, he shows no sign of snuffles," Dad assured him. "But he will need dental treatment very soon. Has he been off his food?"

The boy nodded.

"Yeah, for about a week now."

"I'm not surprised with teeth like that," Dad murmured.

"Will he have to have his teeth out?"

"No, but the overgrown ones will need filing down, under anaesthetic of course," Dad explained. "You must get him to your local vet as soon as possible."

"I will," the boy promised.

At the end of the clinic Dad assured all the pet owners that he hadn't seen a single sign of snuffles in any of the rabbits.

"I'm grateful to all of you for bringing your pets into school. It's better to be safe than sorry," he said. "Now, while I'm here, I'd just like to take this opportunity to run through a few vital tips on caring for your rabbit."

33

The pet owners nodded eagerly.

"Good idea," said a girl at the front.

"Some things might seem a bit obvious to you serious rabbit owners," he said with a warm smile. "But I'll start with the obvious and work my way through to the not so obvious. First of all, rabbits need lots of fresh air which calls for an enclosure or a portable exercise run which can be moved around the garden. Second, a big airy hutch, preferably with two connecting compartments. One, for the daytime, with a mesh door to admit light and air, the other with a fitted door so the rabbit can snuggle up at night, safe from the wind and the rain. I know you're all busy people, doing your homework as soon as you get in from school," he joked, "but do remember to clean your hutches out regularly and give your rabbits a good balanced diet. They like crushed oats, wheat, rabbit pellets and apples, as well as greens and carrots. Always check they've got enough fresh water, especially in the summer, and take them along to your local vet's for a regular check-up. They can easily spot inflammation of the mouth and

34

overgrown teeth like I've just seen in one of the rabbits here. Also they should be injected against myxomatosis and HVD which is a fatal viral disease. That's about it," he concluded. "Look after your pets and you'll get long years of pleasure from them.'

The pupils thanked Mr Church and filed out of the hall, carrying their rabbit cages with them.

"Thank goodness that's over," cried Jess letting out a huge sigh of relief.

"When I saw that rabbit dribbling I thought we'd got another case of snuffles on our hands," said Beth.

"So did I," Dad admitted. "But I listened long and hard to its chest and it was as clear as a bell so it had to be something else."

"I'd never have thought it was its teeth," said Beth.

Dad nodded.

"I've seen rabbit's teeth grow so long they've locked into the opposite jaw."

"Thank goodness you're a vet, Dad," joked Jess.

"That reminds me," said Dad checking his watch, "we'd better be off, I've got an evening surgery in fifteen minutes."

4

The snow continued through January. It was snow like they'd never seen before. When they'd lived in London, snow fell, turned to slush and disappeared. Here, on the edge of the Pennine moors, it fell in great drifts over a metre high and it stayed for weeks.

These days when they got home from school it was too dark to go out for walks but at weekends they had the best time ever. One frosty bright Saturday morning Beth Mars, who knew the moors like the back of her hand, phoned up and suggested they all went for a hike to High Crags.

"Cool!" Jess instantly agreed. "But we'll have to wait for Luke to get dressed, he's still in his pyjamas!"

The dogs instinctively knew that a walk was in the air.

"Woof! Woof!" they barked at Luke, flaked out on the sofa watching Saturday morning television. Poppy impatiently snuffled his hair and Digger licked his bare feet.

"All right, all right!" cried Luke, leaping off the sofa. "I get the message."

Half an hour later, wrapped in woolly scarves, gloves and hats, the four friends set off into the glittering bright morning. All around them the hills peeled away, rising higher and higher as they melted into the high flanks of the Pennine ridge.

"Magic!" cried Jess as their boots crunched on the snowy path.

The dogs frisked ahead, mad with excitement, as they dived in and out of snow-drifts, chasing rabbit smells. After ten minutes of steady uphill walking they were all hot and itchy under their winter woollies. Anoraks were unzipped, scarves and gloves stuffed into pockets, as they tried to cool themselves down.

"I wish I hadn't put this jumper on," Jess moaned.

"You'll need it when we get on to the higher ground," Beth assured her. "Once we move out of the valley the wind whistles over the tops and it's freezing."

She was right too. As they cleared the protective shelter of Moorside valley the wind hurtled off the Pennines and nearly blew them over. Buffeted and blown they reached the last farm before the wild moors took over. Farmer Bracegirdle waved to them and Mrs Bracegirdle came out for a chat.

"Have you heard about our new arrival?" she asked the visitors.

The blank look that passed between them answered her question.

"Come with me," she said mysteriously.

Curiously they followed her across the farmyard.

"I bet it's a ram!" giggled Beth behind her hand.

"Or a new tractor!" whispered Jess.

Nothing prepared them for the sight that met their eyes when Mrs Bracegirdle swung open the barn door. There, standing in a loose box, was the sweetest little donkey they'd ever seen.

"Dora," cooed Mrs Bracegirdle lovingly. "Isn't she a beauty?"

They were used to Nutty's big, wavy ears, thick coat and cheeky face, and could see that by comparison Dora was smaller in build with enormous big, brown eyes fringed with wonderful long eyelashes. When she saw Mrs Bracegirdle she made gentle little grunting noises as she eagerly nudged her hand for a cuddle.

"She's gorgeous," sighed Jess.

"We think so," said Mrs Bracegirdle fondly.

"Don't let Nutty see her," joked Luke. "It'll be love at first sight."

"Just imagine him trotting up your lane to court Dora," chuckled Jess.

"She'd probably enjoy all the attention," laughed Mrs Bracegirdle.

After ten minutes of stroking and petting Dora they tore themselves away and struck out towards the higher ground leading towards High Crags. Mrs Bracegirdle insisted they each took a flapjack, warm from the oven, to help them along their way.

"Mmm, delicious," mumbled Jess as she swallowed down the last delicious crumb. "I could eat twenty of those."

"Me too," Luke agreed. "Can't we stop soon for our picnic?"

"No," Beth told him firmly. "It's too cold."

"Even if we shelter under a rock?" Luke suggested.

"Much too cold," Beth insisted. "Best to stop at High Crags where we can eat in the abandoned farmhouse."

With the dogs bounding ahead they got their second wind and eased into a steady pace of walking as they absorbed the majestic snowscape all around them.

"It's like walking on top of the world," said Jess. "Look how small everything seems from up here."

Far below them Moorside lay in a fold of the hills, its snowy white blanket broken

41

by a jigsaw pattern of drystone walls and a huddle of stone cottages with smoke pluming from their chimney tops. The sun beamed down on the village, momentarily illuminating the Sanctuary as it flashed overhead.

"It all seems so far away," murmured Jess dreamily.

"Woof! Woof!" barked the dogs from high above.

"Look!" cried Sam, shading his eyes against the glare of the midday sun. "They've reached High Crags."

Quickening their pace they rounded a stone outcrop and gazed at the deserted old farmhouse that lay on the low ridges of the lofty Pennine peaks.

"Now we can eat!" laughed Luke.

High Crags farm, blasted on all sides by the raging wind, had stood derelict for years. Luke and Jess had first seen it in the summertime, with larks rising around it, singing their hearts out. Midwinter told a different story. It was desolate and torn apart by the elements. Loose tiles clattered across the stone floor, sash windows rattled in the broken frames, and a door creaked eerily as it swung from its shattered hinges.

"Spooky," said Jess as she peeped into the dark, gutted rooms. "Can't we eat somewhere else?"

"We could but we'll be sheltered from the wind in here," Beth told her. The sooty hearth gaped like a black hole and an old cooking pot, hanging from a metal bar over the fire, creaked mournfully. They cleared a space on the floor and sat down in a huddle to share out their picnic. Combining their food they finished up with a feast. Chicken sandwiches, cheese and pickle, peanut butter and banana, and pasties, still slightly warm from this morning's baking. They had cartons of orange, plus chocolate fudge slices and satsumas. The dogs ate all the crusts and a spare chocolate slice between them, then sat and watched them eat every single mouthful. Poppy put her paw on Sam's arm and looked at him with her big brown eyes.

"Honestly, you make me feel guilty," laughed Sam as he gave her a bit more cake.

Too full to move they sat and made up stories about who might have lived in the abandoned farmhouse.

"Why would anyone choose to live in this remote part of the moors?" Luke wondered.

"Maybe there was tragedy," said Jess dramatically. "A man or a woman who was thrown out of the village because they didn't fit in, or maybe they did something wrong…" her eyes grew bigger as she got into the story.

"Oh, no! She's off," laughed Luke, well used to Jess's fertile imagination.

"Yes!" cried Beth, warming to the idea. "A white witch perhaps, who'd been accused of some terrible deed and ran away up here to hide."

"Oh, I wish these walls could tell their stories," sighed Jess. "So many things must have happened here over the centuries."

The sharp winter sun going behind the clouds cast a gloomy shadow over the house, sending a shiver through all of them.

"Better keep an eye on the time," said

Beth, checking her watch. "It goes dark really early up here in the winter."

Through the broken roof tiles they could see dark clouds forming outside. Little flakes of snow drifted in and swirled into the dusty corners of the room.

"Let's move," said Luke, rising to his feet. "We don't want to get stuck up here in a snowstorm."

"It could be fun," said Jess who always loved the idea of an adventure.

"I don't think so," shivered Beth.

They quickly gathered up their rubbish and shouldered their rucksacks that were now much lighter.

"Stick together," yelled Sam as they stepped out into the snow.

In single file they set off down the track with the dogs staying close beside them. The snowstorm blew wildly around them, stabbing their eyes with icy flakes as they walked into the full force of it. Moorside had completely disappeared from sight and without Sam and Beth's sure knowledge of the moors Jess and Luke would have been seriously lost. As they lost height the going became significantly easier. The snow still blew around them but they could now shelter under the rocky crags that were strewn along the lower slopes. Suddenly a pale sun broke through the thinning clouds and the track home wound clearly ahead.

"Thank goodness for that," muttered Jess as she shook melting snow out of her anorak hood.

By the time they reached the Bracegirdles' farm the light was fading. Soft lamplight glowed invitingly through the front windows of the farmhouse, illuminating Mrs Bracegirdle bustling about in the kitchen.

"I'm tempted to pop in and ask for another flapjack," laughed Luke.

"Best keep going while the light's good," advised Beth.

About a mile from home the dogs started scuffling frantically about in a deep snow-drift.

"What is it, Digger?" called Jess. "Oh, dear! I hope Poppy's not buried inside the drift."

They all hurried forwards and called anxiously.

"Poppy! Digger! Get out of there."

A minute passed and Poppy came out, wagging her tail excitedly. Digger followed slowly behind her, gently carrying something in his big, soft mouth.

"What on earth has he got?" cried Luke.

In the fast-fading light it was difficult to tell what the large, floppy grey thing was. Digger came right up to them and dropped his find obediently at their feet.

"Oh, no!' cried Jess, covering her face in shock.

Lying on the ground was a large tawny owl, all wet and dishevelled.

"Is it dead?" gasped Beth.

Luke stooped to feel the owl's neck.

"There's a pulse still going." Taking off his fluffy anorak he bundled the tawny owl into it and set off running down the track. "Quick! Before it freezes to death!"

When they got back to the Sanctuary, Mum was in her surgery. She looked astonished when Luke ran in and gently placed the unconscious tawny owl on her treatment table.

"The dogs found it in a snow-drift," he

47

explained breathlessly.

With all of them standing around the table, Mum calmly examined the owl.

"She's been burnt. Look, there are scorch marks on her feet and wings," she said as she held up the claws which were marked with burns.

"How could she possibly get burnt?" Beth puzzled.

"I think she's been electrocuted," Mum replied.

"Poor thing," murmured Beth.

"Electrocuted on what?" asked Luke.

"Overhead cable wires. It's really quite common," Mum told them. "She probably lost her way in the snow and perched on a live cable."

"Will she die?" Jess asked anxiously.

"No," Mum replied. "I'll give her an antibiotic injection right away then you can help me treat her wounds."

After the injection had been administered they smoothed cooling moisturising ointment into the burns then applied wet dressings to the open wounds.

"Won't she need feeding?" asked Sam.

"She's in no state to eat at the moment,"

Mum said. "But I can inject subcutaneous fluids under her skin, that should zap her up." Catching Sam's puzzled expression she added. "It's an injection of glucose which can be quickly absorbed into the body. It'll feed her while she's weak."

By the time they'd finished feeding and cleaning the owl she was beginning to show signs of life.

"Hello," whispered Jess as the owl stared up at them with terrified honey-coloured eyes. "We're just making you better."

The owl panicked and lurched forwards.

"Better get her into a cage before she hurts herself," said Mum as she gently lifted the owl and carried her into a small store-room at the back of the treatment room. "There you go," she murmured as she put the bird into a cage on a shelf. "You'll be better off in here, in the dark, without the glare of all those bright lights." Jess brought a heat lamp which Mum hung over the cage to keep the owl warm. "Have a good night's sleep, then we'll give you something proper to eat for breakfast," she whispered as she firmly closed the store-room door behind her.

"Owls like mice and shrews," Jess said knowingly.

"She'll have to make do with rabbit meat," Mum replied.

"How will you get it down her?" asked Sam.

"We'll wrap bits of it in fluff and she'll wolf it back." Mum laughed at Sam's disgusted expression. "You can lend a hand if you want," she teased.

Sam shook his head.

"I don't think I fancy that," he said with a grimace.

5

The following week two significant things happened. The owl was released back on to the moor where it cautiously spread its wings then took off into the sky with a loud shriek. The second less joyful event was Nutty disappearing.

On Wednesday morning when Jess opened the door to give Nutty his breakfast she found the stable completely empty. She raced back into the house, white with shock.

"He's gone!" she spluttered.

The assembled family stared at her.

"Who's gone where?" Luke demanded.

"NUTTY!" Jess shouted. "He isn't in his stable."

As a body they leapt up from the table and ran across the yard to the empty stable.

"Maybe he's gone for a walk," said Daisy.

"He might be in the garden," cried Danny hopefully.

Nutty was nowhere to be found.

"I'm not going to school until he comes home," Jess cried, near to tears.

"Nonsense," Mum said briskly. "He's bound to turn up. After all a donkey can't go far in this weather."

Reluctantly they all set off for school, scouring every lane and meadow along the way. Even on the school bus they continued to look down the roads they passed. Jess couldn't concentrate on a thing during her double maths period and at the end of it she got a severe ticking off from the teacher.

"I'm going to phone home," she told Beth as the break bell rang. Borrowing a coin from Luke she dialled the familiar numbers with shaking hands. Dad answered.

"Moorside Animal Sanctuary," he said smoothly.

"Dad!" cried Jess. "It's me."

"Hi, me," Dad teased.

Jess ignored his silly joke and asked breathlessly, "Is he back?"

"Yes. He came trotting back about ten minutes ago, wet through and starving hungry."

"Oh!" Jess gasped in relief. "Is he OK?"

"He's fine but we've no idea where he disappeared to," Dad replied. "Bit of a mystery really."

Before Jess could ask another question the line went dead.

"Well at least he's back," sighed Jess as she replaced the receiver. "Let's hope he doesn't pull another disappearing trick like that again."

Nutty did. The next morning, and the morning after. In fact every morning that week. By Saturday Jess and Luke were determined to get to the bottom of the mystery.

"I'm going to find out where he goes if I have to sleep in the barn to follow him," Luke said.

"We'll *have* to sleep in the barn," Jess reasoned. "We'll never hear him escape if we're upstairs in the house asleep in our bedrooms."

Mum and Dad couldn't believe their ears when they announced their plan to sleep out in the barn.

"You've got to be joking," said Mum incredulously.

"It's the end of January. Freezing," Dad added.

"We've got excellent sleeping bags," Luke pointed out. "And there's all that straw in the barn, that's a good insulator against cold."

"It's only one night," Jess pleaded. "It might solve the mystery. After all we can't go on forever not knowing where Nutty disappears to."

Mum and Dad looked at each other and shrugged.

"OK," Dad said. "Give it a whirl and see what happens."

Armed with flasks, torches, sandwiches, crisps, chocolate and hot water bottles, Jess and Luke settled down in the snug barn opposite Nutty's stable. The twins were *desperate* to join in but Jess and Luke refused point-blank to let them share the adventure.

"No way," said Luke bluntly. "You're too young."

It was exactly the kind of comment that was guaranteed to wind the twins up.

"Says *who*?" snapped Danny furiously.

"Says *me*!" Luke replied.

"And who are you to say what we can do?" fumed Daisy. "Mum and Dad are in charge of us, not you, big-head!"

Luke, who could never be bothered with protracted arguments, walked off with a dismissive, "Grow up, you two!"

Left alone with Jess the twins tried a different tack.

"*Please*, Jess," they wheedled.

"No way!" she exclaimed. "We're trying to solve a mystery not organize a party."

"We'll be good," Daisy promised with her cutest smile.

"*No*!" Jess replied flatly. "It'll be too

noisy if we're all out in the barn. We'll start arguing, or giggling," she added realistically. "And in the middle of it Nutty will do a runner and none of us will even notice."

"Rat!" yelled the twins and stormed off in a mega huff.

On Friday night Jess and Luke set up their make-shift camp in the barn and watched Nutty at extremely close quarters. After his supper he snuffled about in his stable, inspecting every nook and cranny for any tasty left-over morsels then he licked his feed bucket for the fifth time and finally gave it an impatient kick and sent it flying into the corner.

"So that's how his feed bucket finishes up over there every night," chuckled Jess.

Once Nutty had decided there was absolutely no food to be had he popped his head over his stable door and stared dreamily up at the dark starry sky. Sniffing the sharp, frosty air he sighed then, grunting and groaning, he settled himself down on his warm bed of straw.

"He's so funny," giggled Jess.

"Shsh!" hissed Luke. "We don't want him to know we're near."

To stop herself from laughing, Jess stuffed some chocolate into her mouth and stared out at the sky where puffs of clouds were slowly obliterating the bright stars.

"I think there might be more snow," she said as she snuggled deep into her sleeping bag.

"Good," said Luke. "A light fall of snow will make it easy for us to follow Nutty's footsteps."

"You're a regular Sherlock Holmes," mocked Jess.

Luke ignored her teasing and said, "We should sleep in turns,"

"Good idea," Jess agreed. "I'll do the first watch."

"Right," said Luke, settling down for the night.

But sleep didn't come that easy. Mice scuttled under the hay bales, owls hooted as they hunted on the moors and Nutty snored his head off! By midnight neither of them had been to sleep.

"I'm starving!" whispered Jess.

"Time for a midnight feast," said Luke,

reaching out for his rucksack.

As snowflakes swirled outside the barn they tucked into hot chocolate, cheese sandwiches and crisps.

"That's better," yawned Jess.

"I'll watch, you sleep," said Luke, forcing himself to keep his eyes open.

Within five minutes he was fast asleep. Outside the moon sailed out from behind the clouds and gilded the sleeping pair in moonshine.

At dawn Jess, who was the lightest sleeper of the two, suddenly awoke to a persistent rattling sound. Momentarily confused she looked around then nudged Luke awake.

"I can hear something," she whispered.

Shivering with cold they slipped out of their sleeping bags and crept to the door where they could see Nutty with his head over the stable door.

"What's he doing?" muttered Luke.

It didn't take long to find out. Five minutes later Nutty shot the bolt of his stable door and trotted briskly into the cobbled yard.

"How did he do that?" gasped Jess.

"With his teeth!" whispered Luke as incredulous as she was. "Quick, grab your boots and follow him."

By the time they'd scrambled into their boots and anoraks Nutty had disappeared from sight.

"Oh, no!" cried Jess, looking desperately around. "We've lost him."

"No, we've not," laughed Luke as he ran after Nutty's tracks in the newly fallen snow. "Follow the hoof prints!"

Nutty's prints led them out on to the open moors. Higher and higher they climbed, getting hotter and hotter as they ran up the snowy tracks following him.

"Maybe he's gone to Farmer Smethurst's," said Jess hopefully.

Nutty's footsteps didn't take a right into the Smethurst farm, they just carried straight on up.

"I hope he's not gone all the way up to High Crags," Luke said, puffing and blowing with exertion.

Fear drove them on, making them trip and slither on the icy paths as they imagined all the dangers Nutty might be in. The sun, rising fast in a sky that rapidly changed from pearl to lilac to azure, shone down and started to soften the tracks Nutty had made.

"Quickly!" shouted Luke as he broke into a run. "Before Nutty's footprints disappear!"

Sweating and gasping for breath they reached Farmer Bracegirdle's farm where to their astonishment Nutty's prints led straight down the track leading to the barn.

"Heck! You're up early," called Farmer Bracegirdle from the other side of a drystone wall. "What brings you here?"

"We're looking for our donkey," Jess explained.

Farmer Bracegirdle took one look at their hot, flushed faces and burst out laughing.

"Well I've heard a lot of daft excuses but yours takes the biscuit. Looking for your donkey indeed," he chuckled.

From across the field came a loud "Eee-aww".

"There goes Dora calling for her breakfast," said the farmer.

No sooner were the words out of his

mouth than another "Ee-aww" rang out.

"That doesn't sound like our Dora," he added with a frown.

"No, but it does sound like our Nutty!" cried Luke.

Running as fast as they could they belted down the path, straight past Mrs Bracegirdle who was feeding the chickens in the yard. She looked up in astonishment as Luke and Jess waved and whizzed by. They found the barn door up and Jack and Tara Bracegirdle inside.

"Hiya!" called Tara. "Look who we've got here…"

Nutty and Dora were standing close together, nibbling each others ears.

"Nutty!" gasped Luke and Jess in relief.

The naughty donkey gave them such an indignant look, as if to say, who invited *you* here?

"They've been courting all week," Tara announced.

"How do you know?" asked Luke suspiciously.

"We've seen them," Jack replied.

"And you never said a word to anybody?" Jess exclaimed. "We've been worried sick."

"We didn't want to spoil it," Tara confessed. "We thought they might make babies."

"Might make babies!" cried Mrs Bracegirdle walking into the barn.

Seeing their parents, Jack flashed a warning look at his sister who carried on oblivious of the shock waves she was creating.

"Nutty comes here every morning," she continued blithely.

"How does he get through the barn door?" Luke demanded.

"Oh, we open it for him," Tara told him.

"You little monkeys!" giggled Mrs Bracegirdle. "You shouldn't have done that."

"But they *really* like each other," cried Tara. "Look at them."

There was no doubt at all as to how much the donkeys liked each other. Nibbling and licking, they couldn't leave each other alone!

"We stayed up all night to find out where Nutty runs off to," Jess told the children.

Mrs Bracegirdle shook her head in disbelief.

"How on earth does he get here?" she asked.

"He shoots the bolt to his stable door and trots over the moors. We've seen him do it," Jess explained. "Now we know why," she added with a smile.

Luke was staring hard at Tara and Jack as another thought dawned.

"So how does he get back home again?" he asked.

The two culprits shuffled guiltily.

"Well..." Jack started nervously.

"Go on," urged Mrs Bracegirdle.

"When we give Dora her breakfast we don't give any to Nutty," Jack confessed.

"He doesn't like that," giggled Tara.

"We thought if we fed him he'd never go home," Jack said. "He hangs around for a while then gets fed up and heads off down the track towards the Sanctuary."

"The cheek of you Nutty," laughed Jess.

"It's the only way to make him leave," Tara explained. "He's so hungry he *has* to go home."

"But how did he know Dora was here in the first place?" Luke puzzled. "It's not like he can smell her half-way down the valley."

"There's no point in trying to be logical when it comes to animals," said Farmer Bracegirdle with a shrug. "I mean, how do birds know exactly when to migrate in the autumn? They just do. It's as simple as that."

Jess patted Nutty fondly.

"Naughty boy," she murmured. "We've been worrying all week while you've been gadding about up here."

Nutty looked up with dreamy eyes then returned to nibbling Dora's mane.

"And we never knew a thing," said Mrs Bracegirdle.

"How could we if Tara and Jack were keeping it a secret from us?" the farmer pointed out.

With the mystery finally solved, Luke and Jess set off with Nutty, leading him on a head collar and lead rope they borrowed from the Bracegirdles. As soon as the twins heard the clip-clop of hooves in the cobbled yard they came tearing out of the house, agog to hear where he'd been. They asked about twenty questions without pausing for breath once.

"Where's he been?"

"How did you find him?"

"What did he do?"

"Hold it, hold it," cried Luke. "Let's put Nutty in his paddock and feed him then we'll answer your questions over breakfast."

"Dead right," sighed Jess weakly. "I'm famished."

After they'd polished off scrambled eggs, mushrooms and sausages Jess and Luke sat back in their chairs and explained that naughty Nutty had fallen in love!

"Your friends Tara and Jack Bracegirdle had a lot to do with it," laughed Jess. "They more or less introduced them!"

"You should see them together," chuckled Luke. "Love's young dream."

Mum and Dad exchanged an amused look.

"There could be repercussions, you know," said Dad with a wry smile.

"Dora's in season," Mum added. "I should know, I examined her only the week before last."

There was a stunned silence broken only by the clatter of Jess's knife and fork as it slipped from her fingers.

65

"Do you mean…?" she gulped.

"Nutty could be a father!" squeaked Daisy, going red in the face.

"That's exactly what I mean," said Mum. "Not right away of course," she quickly added. "In about a year's time."

The twins sighed rapturously.

"Nutty and Dora," whispered Daisy dreamily. "Awww…"

6

A month later Mum drove up to the Bracegirdles' farm and did a pregnancy test on Dora.

"Your donkey's going to be a mum," she told Tara and Jack, who were standing with Danny and Daisy, watching Mrs Church's every move.

"Brilliant!" whooped Jack.

"Wait till we tell Nuts," laughed Daisy.

"When?" asked Tara excitedly.

"Oh, not until early January, next year," Mum replied.

"What a *long* time," complained Tara.

"You can't hurry nature," smiled Mum. "It takes a long time to grow a foal."

"Imagine Dora's little foal," enthused Daisy. "It'll be so sweet."

"Not if it's got Nutty's great big ears," teased Danny

"I wonder if it'll be a girl or a boy?" said Jack.

"You'll know in ten months," Mum replied.

Dora impatiently kicked her feed bucket, as if to say, fill it up, I'm eating for two!

With the snow gone and the worst of the winter weather behind them the builders pushed on with the final stage of the large animal hospital.

One bright spring afternoon Luke and Jess got home from school to find the scaffolding that had surrounded the building for months had been taken down. The new large animal hospital, built of weathered Yorkshire stone, was revealed in all it's glory.

"Wowee!" gasped Jess. "I never imagined it would look this good."

"Can you take us round, Mum?" Luke asked Mrs Church as she dashed by.

"I wish I could," she replied. "But I'm late for my surgery. Sorry," she added regretfully. "Ask Beryl, she might spare you ten minutes."

Beryl didn't need to be asked twice.

"I'm so excited about the hospital," she raved. "State of the art technology. Just fabulous!"

Chatting excitedly, they were crossing the yard when the twins ran up.

"Where are you going?" they yelled.

"For a quick tour round the hospital now that the been taken scaffolding's down," Beryl explained.

"Can we come?" begged Daisy.

"Preferably not," said Luke who was often irritated by the twins endless stream of questions.

"Tough, we are," said Danny in a voice that meant he wasn't going to be put off.

"You can all come," said Beryl in her good-natured way. "But no wandering off on your own. The electricians and carpenters are still finishing off so watch your step and don't trip over any loose wires," she added as she unlocked the door.

Though they'd all poured over the architect's plans many times and they'd seen the hospital going up right under their noses none of them were quite prepared for what they now walked into. Even unfurnished the hospital was staggeringly impressive

"Amazing!" cried the twins as they looked around in astonishment.

"Right, let's start here, where it all begins," said Beryl thoroughly enjoying herself. "The sick animals arrive in their horse boxes which are parked out there," she waved towards the end of the yard where a huge turning area had been marked out. "They are brought in through here," she said, pushing open enormously wide double doors that were about four metres high.

"A giraffe could get in here without any problem," said Danny excitedly.

"What if the animal's so sick it can't walk?" asked Daisy.

"See!" exclaimed Luke. "Didn't I say we'd

get earache if these two pains came along."

"It's all right," soothed Beryl. "They're just curious. If the animal's too sick to stand then it will have to be hoisted into the hospital," she explained to Daisy. "They're brought into here," she said, leading them to an open space. "This is the clinic hall, the centre of the entire building, all the other rooms lead off from here – the nurses' station, the holding box, the induction box, the operating theatre, the sterile prep rooms and the recovery boxes. Come and look at my nurses' station. Sounds dead posh, doesn't it?" she giggled.

They walked into a room lined with shelves and cupboards.

"This is where everything will be stored. Drugs, bandages, plasters, syringes, needles, the lot. There'll be computers in here too, sterilizing units, washing machines and tumble dryers for laundering theatre gowns, and theatre drapes. A fridge and a freezer for storing drugs, plasma, vaccines and sterile bacterial swabs."

"What's this for?" yelled the twins from the clinic hall.

"Don't touch anything," Luke snapped as he strode off after them.

"We're not touching, we're looking," Danny pointed out.

"That's the stocks," said Beryl standing by a metal pen. "It's for holding animals during an examination. It's adjustable," she said as she moved the metal bars up and down, "so we can fit in any animal, no matter how tall or fat they are."

"Is this the operating theatre?" asked Jess, walking into an enormous room with huge double doors that went almost up to the ceiling.

"No, that's the holding room," Beryl told her. "This is where the animals are prepared for surgery."

"Won't they be frightened?" Jess said.

"They're sedated before they're even brought in here," Beryl explained. "This is where we clean out their feet, shave the area to be operated on and give them a mouthwash."

"Why?" asked Jess.

"To swab out their throat before we insert the oxygen tube which will be used during the op," Beryl told her. "After that they're led across the hall area into the induction box."

The twins ran ahead, into the box, and stopped in amazement as their feet hit the spongy floor.

"Cool!" they yelled as they bounced up and down.

"It's padded from top to bottom," Beryl told them.

"Why?" asked Daisy.

"Because in this box the patient is given two sedative injections – one which makes them dopey and another which makes them drop to the ground. That's why the entire box is padded, to protect their fall."

"Poor things," sighed tender-hearted Jess.

"Isn't it dodgy when they fall?" asked Luke. "I mean, couldn't they break something when they go down?"

"They could if the fall wasn't controlled," Beryl said. "The drugs make them floppy so it's possible to guide them down. The idea is they fold rather than fall."

"Cor, you must be strong," said Daisy, her eyes wide with admiration.

"Just call me Superwoman!" teased Beryl, as she flexed the muscles in her arms.

"So how do you get the unconscious animals out of here?" asked Luke intrigued by the design of the building.

"That hoist up there tracks along to the operating theatre," Beryl said, pointing to a hoist that ran along a yellow track in the ceiling. "It's electrically operated by this," she said showing them a large control pad, lined with buttons. "Press that green button," she said, holding the pad out to Danny who did as she instructed. The hoist tracked along the ceiling then smoothly descended to their level. "Try the red one," she told Daisy. With a flick of the switch the hoist moved up then tracked out of the induction box, across the ceiling of the clinic and into the operating theatre.

"That's ingenious!" gasped Jess.

"Can it take any load?" Luke asked.

"Any load that we need," Beryl assured him. "A horse is about five to six hundred kilos. It could take more than that if necessary."

The operating theatre was bare apart from a hydraulically operated padded table in the centre.

"Is that big enough for a cow or a bull?"

puzzled Jess as she stared at the table.

"It's big enough for anything!" laughed Beryl, fitting metals sections on to the table, "It can go wider, longer, lower, higher. You could get a rhino on it, at a push!"

"What happens after the operation?" asked Danny eagerly.

"The patient's hoisted out and taken to one of the recovery boxes. There are two, one on either side of the clinic."

They followed her into a recovery box which like the induction box was padded from floor to ceiling.

"Why is it smaller than the other box?" asked Jess.

"The size restricts the animal from throwing itself around as it comes out of the anaesthetic," Beryl explained. "Horses are the worst. They often panic as the anaesthetic wears off and charge at the wall. Sometimes they break a leg, or worse and have to be put down."

"Poor things," said Jess. "Imagine going through an operation then breaking a leg."

"That's why recovery boxes are small, it restricts their movements," Beryl said.

"Can you see inside the box once the animal's in here?" asked Danny.

"Yes, come out and I'll show you," said Beryl as she closed the doors behind them. "Now look through the viewing window and you'll see a mirror, up there on the wall inside the box."

Danny stood on his tiptoes.

"That's clever," he said excitedly. "I can see inside from every angle."

"We can shut the doors and leave the animals alone but still monitor their progress by watching the mirror. There's a heater up there on the other wall," she pointed out. "To keep the patients warm after their ops."

"You've thought of *everything*," said Jess, totally impressed.

"Not me, love. It was your Mum and the architect. They're the brilliant ones. "Come on, we'll go out the back way."

On their way out they passed the X-ray room and the theatre prep area.

"When we're doing ops this will be a completely sterile area and nobody will be allowed in unless they're gowned up, scrubbed up and wearing a mask."

"Why?" asked Danny.

"To cut down the risk of infection during the operations," Beryl replied.

Out in the yard was an intensive care unit with three boxes and further along was a mother and baby unit.

"It's a loose box that can be divided up into a large pen for the mother and a smaller one for the baby," Beryl explained.

"Perhaps Dora will have her foal in here," said Daisy excitedly.

"I hope not," Beryl exclaimed. "This is a critical care mother and baby unit. Dora's a young, healthy donkey. With a bit of luck she'll have her foal in Farmer Bracegirdle's barn, believe me. Watch out for the loose wires out there," she called to the twins who were in the prep room outside.

"When will everything be completely finished?" asked Daisy.

"Easter," Beryl replied.

Luke quickly counted on his fingers.

"That's only three weeks away. Will everything really be ready by then?"

"It'll *have* to be," chuckled Beryl. "Otherwise the television company and the press won't be very impressed."

"Are they coming?" cried Danny.

"Everybody's coming to the grand opening of the Sanctuary Animal Hospital!" laughed Beryl.

In the middle of all the frenzied building work Poppy came into season. By the time it became really obvious, Digger and Poppy had been seen mating twice. First by Jess and then by Danny.

"Oh, no!" cried Mum when she heard the news. "It's the worst possible timing."

"But you always said they could have puppies one day," Jess reminded her.

"Yes," Mum agreed. "But not now!"

"You're the vet," Danny teased. "You should know about these things."

"I *do* know about these things," Mum laughed. "They just weren't on my mind at the moment. Are you *sure* you saw them mating?" she asked.

"They were *really* mating when I saw them out in the garden," Danny said with relish.

"Absolutely," Jess replied.

"There's no point in worrying about it now," Dad said realistically. "The deed's well and truly done."

"Honestly," exclaimed Mum. "We should change the name of this place from the Sanctuary to Animals Galore!"

7

One weekend, just after the clocks had gone forward and the evenings were a little longer, Mum asked Luke and Jess to take some ointment over to Miss Booth, the rare pig breeder, who lived on the far side of the valley.

"I didn't know there was a rare pig breeder in the valley," said Luke.

"Neither did I until she called me the other day to ask if I'd examine her lovely

Gloucester Old Spot who's in farrow."

"Does that mean pregnant?" asked Beth who'd dropped in to help Jess sweep out the kennels.

Mum nodded her head.

"In Rosie's case *hugely* pregnant," she laughed.

"Do you think we might get to see her when we take the ointment over?" Jess asked.

"You might if you ask politely," Mum said. "But don't nag Miss Booth. She prefers her pigs to humans and if she thinks you might upset her babies she'll give you a mouthful."

Luke pocketed the jar of ointment.

"We'll drop it off after our picnic at Smugglers' Hole," he said.

"Thanks," said Mum. "In return I'll pack you an extra-specially big picnic."

"It's a deal!" he answered.

When the dogs saw the rucksack being packed they raced to the back door and sat, excitedly wagging their tails.

"Who said you could come, little fat Poppy?" teased Beth as she stroked the bitch's jet black silky ears. Poppy thumped her tail even harder and licked Beth's nose. "Expectant mums should put their feet up and not go tearing around the moors," Beth added. Poppy scratched at the door, as if to say, just you try keeping me in!

The wind was fresh and brisk, bending the long-stemmed daffodils that strewed the lower foothills. Pale yellow primroses peeped in bright clusters from the hedgerows which dripped with catkins and pussy willow. Larks rose up in front of them, in an ecstasy of spring song, flinging themselves into an arching blue sky. New lambs were everywhere, baa-ing and bleating, as they gambolled wildly in the sunshine. Striking out to the right they followed a narrow track that peeled across the sweeping valley. "Get the dogs on a lead," Sam warned as Poppy and Digger stopped to stare at a ram with curling horns.

Reluctantly the dogs were put on their leads and walked obediently to heel until they were well clear of the sheep. Digger shook himself briskly when his lead was taken off. Poppy sat down and yawned.

"When are her puppies due?" asked Sam as he patted her chubby tummy.

"Sometime in June," Luke replied.

"I bet they'll be gorgeous," sighed Beth. "I wish I could have one."

"You can," Jess cried. "We'll save the best for you."

Luke quickly jabbed her in the ribs.

"I don't think we can afford a Labrador puppy," Beth answered self-consciously.

"Big mouth!" Luke whispered as the other two walked on ahead.

Jess hung back, furious with herself. How could she have opened her big mouth and put her foot in it like that? She knew Mrs Mars had difficulty making ends meet, even though she worked six days a week in the village post office.

"I'm sorry," she whispered when she caught up with Beth.

"Don't worry," said Beth warmly. "Since you moved to Moorside I've got more animals to look after than I've ever had in my life!"

Smiling with relief Jess carried on, squelching over the soggy higher ground running with rivulets of melted snow. The stream gurgled loudly as it bounced over boulders worn smooth with rushing water. They stopped briefly to dip their hot faces into an icy cold pool.

"I've never tasted water like this," said Luke gulping down mouthfuls.

"Natural spring water cooled by Pennine snow," said Sam poetically.

"You sound like a television commercial," giggled Beth.

It was a relief to get to Smugglers' Hole, an enormous upright slab of black rock which rose majestically, sheer on all sides. It looked impenetrably high but there was a secret entrance to the side, a slit less than a metre wide, where somebody slender could slip through. They entered the dark, dank interior which echoed with the steady drip-drip of falling water.

"This place is so s-c-a-r-y," said Beth with a delicious shiver. "I think it's haunted with the ghosts of long-dead smugglers."

"Rotting highwaymen," Sam said. "Who came in here to hide from the customs men and died of pistol wounds."

A falling shower of stones at the back of the cave made them all jump sky-high.

At the sound of the noise, the dogs scampered off into the darkness, barking loudly at imaginary shadows.

"I'm getting out of here," said Beth, making a dash for the narrow gap where a thin strip of blue sky pierced the gloom.

Out in the bright sunshine they laid out their food on a row of small rocks that made a natural table.

"Gorgeous!" sighed Sam, tucking into chicken sandwiches and jam doughnuts. "I bet highwaymen never had grub like this!"

An hour later they started the steep descent down from Smugglers' Hole, following the course of Smugglers' Gill waterfall which tumbled and roared so loudly it drowned out all other sounds. At the base of the fall the dogs ran along a narrow ledge that was curtained off by crashing water. They came out, sleek and wet as black otters, and shook water all over the children. The fall roared into a deep rocky pool that was as clear as crystal then rushed out, into a noisy surging stream which could be crossed at strategic points along the river bank.

It was nearly three by the time they got to Miss Booth's rare breed farm and they could smell the pigs before they even saw them.

"Well pongy," laughed Luke as he held his nose.

Miss Booth came out to meet them, big and broad in muddy dungarees and green wellies.

"You must be the Churches!" she boomed.

"We're Sam and Beth Mars," Beth said quickly. "From Moorside post office."

Miss Booth nodded curtly.

"Like pigs?" she demanded.

They all smiled enthusiastically.

"Excellent! Follow me."

Striding ahead, Miss Booth led them into a charming old-fashioned farm yard lined with red-brick pig pens.

"These are my farrowing sows, the rest of my pigs are out in the meadow," she explained.

In the first pen was a hairy, black Vietnamese pot-bellied pig. She was lying on her side and latched on to every teat running down her belly were lots of tiny, squirming pot-bellied piglets.

"Darling Mao," crooned Miss Booth. "So patient with your greedy brood, aren't you dear?" Mao grunted in reply then serenely returned to the business in hand.

In the next pen was a *vast* saddleback sow snoring blissfully in the sunshine.

"Arabella," whispered Miss Booth. "Best not to disturb her right now. Her babies are due any day and she needs all the sleep she can get."

The visitors smiled at each other conspiratorially as Miss Booth crept silently away to the sound of Arabella's soft snores.

"Here's Rosie," beamed Miss Booth as they came to the last pen in the line, "my precious Gloucester Old Spot, due to farrow in two weeks."

Rosie was as keen on her mistress as she was on her. She lumbered to her feet at the sound of her voice and waddled majestically over, grunting rapturously. As Miss Booth patted Rosie's big, broad head Luke suddenly saw a fleshy, red sack hanging out of the back of the pig. He quickly nudged Jess who followed his gaze and saw it too. With a look of alarm on her

88

face she whispered, "Tell her!"

"Er, Miss Booth," Luke started. "I think there might be something wrong with Rosie."

The pig breeder glared at him indignantly.

What?" she barked.

Luke gulped and pointed nervously towards Rosie's rear end. Miss Booth darted around to the side of the fence where he was standing and gazed in horror at Rosie.

"Oh, my goodness!" she gasped. "Something's dreadfully wrong." Staring wildly at Luke she added, "Go into the house and phone your mother. Tell her we're bringing Rosie down *right away*! The rest of you can help me get her into the trailer."

"B-b-but, Miss Booth," Jess gasped. "She's far too big to go in the Sanctuary surgery."

"I know that!" exclaimed Miss Booth. "But your mother's got a brand spanking new hospital – she can go in there."

"It's not finished yet. The painters and carpenters are just—"

89

Jess never reached the end of her explanation.

"Who cares about blooming painters and carpenters? My darling girl needs attention. Quick now," she snapped at Luke. "Go and make that phone call."

Leaving Miss Booth backing up her trailer Luke dashed into the kitchen where he grabbed the phone and with trembling hands dialled the Sanctuary. He gasped with relief when he heard Beryl's familiar voice.

"Beryl, it's me! I'm at Miss Booth's and her pregnant Gloucester Old Spot sow has something really nasty hanging out of the back of her."

"Describe it as best you can," the nurse urged.

"Well, it's all red and slimy and fleshy, like a big bag," Luke said, desperately searching around for the right words to describe what he'd seen.

"Mm, that sounds like a prolapsed womb to me," murmured Beryl. "Tell Miss Booth that I'll contact your mum on the mobile and she'll be there as soon as possible."

"Beryl!" Luke interrupted her. "Miss Booth's bringing Rosie over to the new hospital *now*!"

"She can't! Tell her to hang on and wait for Mrs Church," Beryl told him firmly.

Luke's reply was drowned out by the sound of Miss Booth blasting her horn outside the kitchen window.

"Hop in!" she bellowed.

Luke put the phone down and ran to the door.

"Our veterinary nurse says you're to wait for Mum to come here," he cried.

"Wait!" exclaimed Miss Booth going bright red in the face. "Wait for my Rosie to lose all her babies? No way! *No way*!"

Just as Luke was clambering into the driver's cab, Beth had a brainwave.

"Why don't Jess and I run back to the Sanctuary?" she suggested. "It's much quicker across country."

"Jolly good idea," boomed Miss Booth. "You can tell that nurse that I'm on my way, whether she likes it or not!"

The dogs eagerly sprang out of the cab after the girls and they all set off across the moors. Not once did they pause for breath as they ran the mile back to the Sanctuary. The first person they saw was Mrs Church scrambling out of her battered old Land Rover.

"Mum!" yelled Jess, nearly falling over in her haste to reach her. "Miss Booth's—"

"It's OK, Jess," Mum replied as the girls stood breathless before her. "Beryl phoned me on the mobile. What is the woman thinking of?" she added furiously.

"She wants you to treat Rosie in the new hospital," Beth gasped.

"She wouldn't wait, even though we told her the hospital's not finished," Jess added. "There's something *really* wrong with Rosie, Mum. She's got a great big sack thing hanging out of her. It's horrible."

"It's got to be a prolapsed womb," muttered Mum, quickly checking her watch. "How long do you think it'll be before she gets here?"

"Fifteen minutes, at the most," Beth replied.

"Right," said Mum, breaking into a run. "Let's go for it!"

8

Beryl went pale when Mrs Church told her to prepare the new hospital for emergency treatment.

"Can't we use the Sanctuary surgery?" she asked.

"No chance. Rosie will go straight through the floorboards if we take her in there," Mum told her.

"So *where* will we treat her?" asked Beryl flustered.

"The induction box will be fine. The girls can hose it down while you and I hang up the theatre drapes."

"The carpenters are working in the nurses' station," Beryl warned her.

"The more the merrier," laughed Mum.

"Well," chuckled Beryl as they dashed off in all directions. "I suppose it proves one thing – Moorside really *does* need a large animal hospital!"

As the girls hosed and disinfected the induction box, Beryl and Mum hung up the sterile theatre drapes then went off to collect swabs, surgical scrubs, scissors, syringes, sedatives, oxygen and respiratory tubes from the nurses' station. Just as Beryl was wheeling the loaded prep trolley across the clinic hall there was the sound of tyres crunching on the gravel outside.

"She's here!" murmured Jess tensely.

"Scrub up and gown up," Beryl told the girls. "We might need you."

Jess and Beth dashed into the changing-room where they removed all their clothes except their underwear and thrust their arms and legs into cotton overalls.

"Don't forget to put on sterile hats and

masks," said Beryl running in to change too.

The girls laughed at the sight of each other in full surgical dress.

"That pig's not going to get infected on account of us," giggled Jess.

Mum was outside in the parking area, helping Miss Booth and the boys to lower the ramp of the trailer. Rosie staggered to her feet and waddled uncomfortably forwards.

"There, there, dear," soothed Miss Booth as they shepherded Rosie in using pig boards to stop her escaping.

"Take her into the induction box," Mum instructed. "Beryl will check her blood pressure and clean her down while I scrub up."

Miss Booth seemed calmer now that Rosie was in safe hands, nevertheless she watched Beryl with a beady eye, especially when she produced a bucket of iodine scrub liquid.

"I've got to wash down the surgical area, Miss Booth," Beryl explained. "It's been exposed to a lot of dirt and we wouldn't want that going into the wound, would we?"

"Absolutely," boomed Miss Booth. "Scrub away, dear girl."

Using large pieces of thick gauze Beryl washed all the dirt off the fleshy bag then took a syringe filled with the iodine scrub and used it to jet off the smaller bits still clinging on.

"Right you two," she said, addressing the girls who were watching wide-eyed from behind their masks. "I want you to stand at either side of Rosie's rear end and lift the surgical drape up so that you're holding the prolapsed womb inside it." Gingerly the girls did as she instructed. "Hold it tight!" Beryl said sharply. "I don't want it anywhere near the floor now I've swabbed it down ready for surgery."

The womb inside the drape was heavy, like holding a plastic carrier bag full of water. Both girls were relieved to see Mrs Church reappear, masked and gowned. After carefully examining the pig she turned to Miss Booth and said calmly, "It's as I thought, a prolapsed womb."

"OH!" cried the owner. "Will she lose the piglets?"

"No," Mum reassured her. "I can push the womb back in and do a purse string suture around the vulva. That should hold it firm until she goes into labour. We need to get to work quickly," she added, "so if you'd wait outside we'll sedate her and get on with it."

Miss Booth reluctantly left and Beryl closed the door behind her. Three tense faces immediately appeared in the viewing window, Miss Booth flanked by Luke and Sam.

"Shall we go?" whispered Jess from behind her surgical mask.

"No, we might need you, but keep quiet," Mum replied. "Ready with the sedative, Beryl?"

The nurse nodded as she filled a syringe from a phial of clear liquid. She handed the syringe to Mum then, talking soothingly, she gently held Rosie's head as Mrs Church injected the pig in the neck. Seconds later the muscle relaxant in the sedative kicked in and with a heavy sigh Rosie crumpled slowly on to her side.

"Good," said Mum. "Let's get to work."

Quickly and efficiently she tucked the

bulging prolapsed womb back into Rosie then, holding on to it with one hand to keep it firmly in place, she took the suture needle and nylon tape from Beryl and stitched a purse string suture around the now stretched opening. When the stitches completely enclosed the vulva, Mum withdrew her hand from inside Rosie and Beryl tightened the sutures.

"Now for a nice big bow," said Mum, tying off the circle of stitches.

"Are you really tying a bow?" asked Beth.

"Yes," Mum replied. "A big one that I can quickly undo when she goes into labour. There, all done!" she said proudly.

"Not quite," said Beryl urgently. "She's contracting. Look, you can see her straining!"

Even in her drowsy state Rosie was indeed straining against the newly placed sutures.

"We'll have to give her an epidural injection to numb her hindquarters," said Mum.

The girls watched breathlessly as Mum carefully and skilfully introduced a long spinal needle into the pig's cord, just above her tail base. When she was happy the needle was correctly placed she released a couple of milligrams of local anaesthetic and Rosie instantly stopped contracting.

"Phew," sighed Jess. "What a relief."

When the operation was completed, Mum went out to talk to Miss Booth leaving Beryl to clean up Rosie's wound.

"She is seriously enormous," said Beryl as she wiped the pig down. "I bet she's got eight little Gloucester Old Spots jumping about inside her."

"I hope they'll be all right," fretted Beth.

"They should be," Beryl assured her. "We'll keep an eye on her in the intensive care unit."

"How are you going to get her there?" asked Beth.

"On a trolley," Beryl explained.

"But we can't lift a pig on to a trolley!" squeaked Beth.

Beryl burst out laughing.

"I know I'm strong love, but even I couldn't do that. Believe it or not there's a hospital trolley built into this floor and

Rosie here happens to be conveniently lying on it. All I've got to do is jack it up and we have one unconscious pig on a trolley!"

To Beth's astonishment Beryl jacked up a section of the induction box floor and there appeared, before her eyes, a hospital trolley.

"Wow!" she gasped. "That's brilliant!"

Half an hour later Rosie was lying on a deep warm litter of straw in one of the hospital's intensive care boxes.

"There, there, my precious," crooned Miss Booth as she squatted on the straw beside her beloved pig. "Mummy must go now," she said regretfully. Rosie looked at her with a trusting expression and grunted drowsily. "You'll call me if there's any change, won't you?" Miss Booth asked Mrs Church.

"Definitely," Mum replied. "We'll keep an eye on her, don't you worry."

"Goodbye, dear," said Miss Booth. "Sleep tight."

With a tender backward glance she left the hospital and they all breathed a huge sigh of relief.

"We did it!" cried Mum, punching the air in triumph. "We performed our first operation in the new hospital!"

"Under pressure," Beryl reminded her with a laugh.

"It looked pretty good to me," said Luke.

"Brilliant!" Jess enthused.

"Why did you call it a purse string suture?" asked Sam.

"The stitches are done in a circle, like a little purse string, so that they can be released instantly when Rosie goes into labour."

"Why?" asked Beth.

"If I have to start unpicking lots of stitches when she's in labour she'll be badly torn. With this technique I give one gentle tug at the bow I left and out pop the piglets."

"Magic," said Sam, clearly impressed.

"Clever," said Luke.

"Come on," said Beryl, quickly ushering everybody out. "Time to leave our patient to sleep off the sedative."

"Night, Rosie," they called softly. "Sleep tight."

9

Early the following morning, when the house was very still and everybody was sleeping, Puss and Boots the kittens came scampering into Luke's bedroom

"Go away," he mumbled as he pushed the mischievous pair off his duvet. "I'm tired."

A combination of the sun shining in through a crack in his curtains and Boots crawling up his back forced Luke out of bed. Once he was up a thought suddenly struck him. Had Rosie had a good night? Slipping into his jeans and a T-shirt he crept downstairs and out of the back door. It was a wonderful spring morning with the birds competing to sing the loudest song. A soft breeze carried the scent of apple blossom on the air and overhead the sky was a dazzling blue.

"I should try getting up at dawn more often!" thought Luke.

Suddenly the morning's beauty was rent by the sound of agonised squealing. Sprinting forwards Luke ran towards the intensive care unit where he found Rosie in the throes of giving birth. Her back end was bulging and she grunted in pain as contractions pushed the swelling further and further out.

"Oh, no!" he gasped.

His first instinct was to run for Mum but, he reasoned, by the time he'd done that the whole of Rosie's back end could be ripped open.

"OK, girl," he said, trying to sound firm when he was in fact shaking all over. "You and I are going to do this together!"

Kneeling down beside the sow he ran a

hand along her heaving sides down to her swollen rear end.

"Where's that bit of nylon tape that Mum left...?" he said, speaking more to himself than to the pig. When his fingers found the tape bow around the purse string suture he grasped it firmly.

"Please, please don't move, Rosie," he murmured.

With sweat pouring out of him Luke took a deep breath and tugged at the stitches. To his overwhelming relief the hole opened wide and with a grateful grunt of relief Rosie sighed and lay back. Moments later the first piglet was born – straight into Luke's hands! One, two, three, four, five more came flying out like little pink bullets. Each was in its own bag which Luke quickly broke open so that the piglets could breathe. He dried each of them off on a clean cloth but he simply couldn't work fast enough. By the time the eighth piglet was born, Luke was sitting in a pool of sticky, slimy fluid frantically trying to clean the tiny squirming bodies. When Jess appeared at the door he cried out with relief.

"Quick, come and help me!"

All in all Rosie had *twelve* healthy piglets. Small and pink with little, stubby ears and tiny tails. They wriggled eagerly towards their mother who was completely out for the count.

"She's still not properly round from the anaesthetic," panicked Jess. "I'm going for Mum."

Five minutes later, Mrs Church rushed into the box and found Luke sitting in the straw, surrounded by piglets.

"How did you do it?" she gasped.

"Easy!" joked Luke. "I tugged the loose thread, just like you said, though I have to admit I was shaking like a leaf, and out they all popped."

"Genius!" exclaimed Mum, bending down to examine Rosie. "Poor old girl. She's had it."

"What about the babies?" asked Jess, anxiously watching the piglets wriggling around their mother's teats. "They need a feed."

"We'll have to take care of them until Rosie comes round," Mum replied. "Stay there."

Five minutes later she returned with a dog cage from the Sanctuary surgery.

"I've sterilized the cage and lined it with an insulating blanket to keep the piglets warm. Pop them inside and we'll get them over to the treatment room."

The three of them carefully put all of the piglets into the dog cage then hurried back to the Sanctuary where Mum put the cage under a heat lamp.

"Now all we've got to do is feed them," said Mum.

"With what?" asked Jess.

"I'll just check," said Mum, flicking through one of her manuals. "A feed mixture of one egg yolk to two cups of milk every two hours," she said, reading aloud from the book.

While Mrs Church prepared the feed, Jess and Luke sterilized the feeding bottles and teats under her supervision.

"You two feed," she instructed. "I'll sterilize and refill the empty bottles."

As soon as the piglets smelt the milk mixture they went *crazy*!

"Here we go," said Luke, lifting out the first and neatly inserting the teat into its open mouth. The piglet latched on to it for dear life and sucked it dry in no time. "I need another bottle," Luke called to Mum as he picked up another hungry piglet. Finally they were all fed, apart from the smallest who lay curled up under the heat lamp.

"The runt," said Mum. "It might be too stressed to feed, or maybe it's just cold," she said, examining the piglet's soft velvety body.

"It mustn't die!" cried Luke.

"Runts often do," Mum told him gently.

"Not this one!" Luke replied. "I brought it into the world and it's not going out right now – no way!"

Seeing Luke's expression, Mum knew he meant it.

"Don't get your hopes up. Life's doesn't always have a happy ending, you know."

As Luke sat cradling the sick piglet Jess cautiously said, "Do you fancy breakfast?"

"No," he replied. "I'm staying here."

"Well, I'm starving," she said, heading for the door.

"Do me a favour, Jess," he called after her. "Bring me over a bacon butty." Suddenly he stopped short and stared at the pitiful little bundle in his hands. "Make it egg on toast!" he said, quickly correcting himself.

Half an hour later Miss Booth rushed into the Sanctuary with her hair flying all over the place and her cardigan on inside out.

"Where are they?" she cried.

"Follow me..." said Beryl with a big smile.

She led her into the prep room where the twelve little piglets were sleeping snugly under the heat lamp. Nose to tail, they looked like a soft pink cushion.

"Oh!" exclaimed Miss Booth and burst into tears. "Perfect," she murmured. "Just perfect."

Suddenly her eyes fell on the runt.

"He's not taken to the bottle," Luke told her. "And Rosie can't feed yet, she's still dozy from yesterday."

"Poor little chap," sighed Miss Booth sadly.

"Luke's determined to pull him through," Beryl told her.

Miss Booth stared at him as if he were a true kindred spirit.

"Luke," she said his name slowly. "Your mother tells me you valiantly delivered all of Rosie's babies and now here you are trying to save her runt. I really am *most* grateful to you, dear boy."

In normal circumstances Luke would have run a mile but these weren't normal circumstances. This was a question of life or death!

"To be honest, Miss Booth, the piglets really delivered themselves once the sutures were out. They shot out like bullets," he told her with a wide grin.

The pig breeder lingered for a few minutes longer over the babies then hurried off to see her adored Rosie. When she'd left the room Luke stared after her.

"It's funny," he said to Beryl. "She seems so grouchy when you first meet her, but she's got a heart of gold and she loves her animals."

"Some people relate better to animals than people," Beryl said then smiled at Luke's thoughtful expression. "Do you know, I think you two have bonded!" she teased.

It was a long stressful day. In between feeds the piglets slept but the runt became visibly weaker. At lunchtime Mum said, "It's been a long morning, Luke. Take a break."

Seeing his mutinous expression she quickly added, "Nothing's going to happen if you disappear for half an hour."

Very reluctantly he dragged himself away from the runt whose rapid breathing seemed shallower than ever.

"Keep an eye on him, Jess," he whispered to his sister as he left.

Jess smiled reassuringly but felt not an atom of hope for the runt's survival.

About quarter of an hour after Luke's departure, just as Jess and Beryl were preparing yet another egg and milk mixture for the ravenous babies, the runt suddenly squeaked. It was the tiniest, most feeble noise Jess had ever heard but it was nevertheless a noise – a real sign of life.

"Beryl!" she gasped. "Did you hear what I heard?"

The nurse didn't answer her question but pointed in amazement to the dog cage where the tiny snuffling runt was crawling blindly over its brothers and sisters.

"I do believe it's missing Luke," whispered Beryl. "Quick, Jess, go and fetch him!"

Jess tore into the house, yelling at the top of her voice.

"LUKE!"

He rushed out of the kitchen, white-faced.

"Is it dead?"

"No, it's moving! It's looking for you," she cried.

Sprinting down the stairs two at a time Luke dashed back to the surgery where incredulously the runt was still wriggling about.

"Give him this," Beryl said as she thrust a feed bottle into his hands.

The piglet instantly calmed down at the touch and smell of Luke and when he put the teat to its tiny gaping mouth it sucked!

"Slowly to start with," warned Beryl. "Give him a breather in between mouthfuls. We don't want him to choke himself."

With infinite care, Luke fed the runt

112

until the bottle was empty then lowered him tenderly back into the cage where he peacefully slept alongside his brothers and sisters. At that touching moment Jess sniggered behind him.

"Blimey, Luke, he thinks you're his mum!"

10

Connor, as Luke named the runt that night, thrived. When Rosie surfaced from the after-effects of her anaesthetic the piglets were immediately returned to her. Grunting and snuffling with pleasure she welcomed her brood back then lay on her side so they'd all have room to latch themselves on to her swollen teats. The whole family watched the moment of reunion through the window of Rosie's box.

115

"Awww…" sighed the twins.

"Check out Connor!" said Luke, proudly watching his baby wriggle in between the other eleven.

"Don't speak too loudly, Luke," Mum said. "If Connor hears your voice it'll distract him from feeding. He has to bond with Rosie now."

Connor did bond with his mum but he loved Luke. He'd only to hear the sound of his approaching footsteps and he'd rush to the door, grunting and squealing in delight. When Luke picked him up for a cuddle he wiggled and squiggled so much it was hard keeping control of him.

"You'll take a nosedive one of these days," Luke laughed as he clutched Connor close. "And flatten that nice little snout of yours."

Miss Booth dropped by every day and she and Luke spent hours together, watching Rosie with her piglets.

"I'd never have thought you'd turn into a pig man," Dad teased.

"I'm not a pig man!" Luke replied indignantly. "I'm a Connor man. Miss Booth says he's a beauty, with real

116

showing potential," he added proudly.

"You do know he'll be going back home soon?" Mum reminded Luke.

"Yes, of course," he replied curtly. "I didn't think he was going to stay here for ever."

Mum and Dad exchanged a glance. They both knew Luke's tough front belied his anxiety over the imminent departure of his beloved Connor.

When the day came for Rosie and her piglets to leave the Sanctuary Luke and Jess drove home with Miss Booth in the trailer.

"I'm so grateful to you both," she said as they bounced over the rutted track to her pig farm. "It makes the separation so much easier for Connor if you're here to settle him."

Luke nodded and smiled politely but Jess could see he wasn't in the least happy about leaving Connor. When they unloaded Rosie into her familiar pig pen she rolled on her back and grunted blissfully. Eleven little piglets rushed around, sniffing out the food trays and water trough, but Connor stood desolately on his own.

"He'll be all right," Jess whispered to

her brother who looked like he was on the verge of tears.

Luke gulped.

"I don't want to leave him," he blurted out.

Jess scrambled around for something comforting to say.

"You'll still be able to see him. He's only a quarter of an hour away."

"It's not the same as seeing him every day and watching him grow up," Luke replied grumpily.

Miss Booth offered them tea but Luke shook his head.

"No thanks," he muttered. "Got to go."

The pig breeder knew Luke too well to be given the brush off.

"I know exactly how you're feeling," she said gently. "Every time I sell one of my dears I feel devastated." She patted Luke's shoulder. "I promise I'll keep you posted on little Connor and you must come and see him as often as you like."

"Thanks, Miss Booth," Luke said and dashed out before his feelings got the better of him.

11

With only days to go before the opening of the animal hospital Mum and Dad were frantically busy. Beryl roped everybody into helping with the last minute preparations.

"The hospital's got to look wonderful," she told Luke, Sam, Jess, Beth and the twins as they all stood in the clinic hall awaiting her instructions.

"But it *is* wonderful!" laughed Danny.

"It's the best."

"I know but I want the whole of the north of England to know it when they see it on telly," Beryl said. "We've got to scrub everything until it shines."

"It's already shining!" laughed Daisy.

"Not *enough*!" Beryl insisted. "Now here's a box of cleaning stuff," she said, shoving cloths and polish into Luke's arms. "Give everything the once over and don't spare the elbow grease."

"The Sanctuary's going to look like a squeaky-clean TV advert," Sam said as he squinted at his own reflection in the changing-room mirror which he'd just polished twice.

"This is television, for real," Luke corrected him. "And all the local press too."

"Plus radio," Jess added, as she swished by with a floor mop. "We're going to put Moorside Sanctuary on the map!"

The day before the opening Miss Booth phoned Luke and said, "I've been thinking, dear. Rosie was the very first patient to be treated in the new hospital and it would be a nice bit of publicity if she were at the

Sanctuary for the opening, don't you think?"

Luke's first reaction was, "Yes!"

"She's living proof of what a good vet your mother is and her appearance would be a great publicity stunt. The media would love it."

"I agree but Mum and Dad would freak out right now if we suggested it," Luke warned her.

"Oh, I wouldn't dream of worrying them with the details," said Miss Booth airily. "I'll just drive the old girl over and we'll secrete her somewhere about the premises."

"Hiding a pig is a big deal, Miss B!" laughed Luke.

"We'll think of something, don't you worry," she replied. "You must come over and see Connor," she added.

"Sure," said Luke but he didn't mean it. He'd visited him twice but the pleasure of seeing him was ruined by the pain of leaving him. Saying goodbye to the piglet standing in the pen staring sadly after him while the other piglets tumbled around in the mud almost broke Luke's heart. It was easier not to see him, and far less painful.

The Sanctuary's open day was from ten till four o'clock on Easter Saturday. The official opening was scheduled for midday so ideally Rosie had to be in place by eleven forty five at the latest. The logistics of hiding a pig in the hospital were just too much for Luke to cope with alone so he took Jess into his confidence.

"You're *what*?" she shrieked.

"It's an excellent idea," he assured her. "Great publicity too."

"But what about Mum and Dad?" she said. "Won't they go mad?"

"They'll only go mad if they know about it," he said. "It's our business to manage the situation so that they don't. Right?"

Jess nodded slowly.

"Right," she said, smiling mischievously. "So, where do we put Rosie once she gets here?"

"Not the clinic hall," said Luke. "It's too big and the public will be walking through there from ten in the morning."

"It's got to be one of the boxes," Jess said thoughtfully.

They both stared blankly at each other then Luke suddenly clicked his fingers.

"The holding box," he exclaimed. "It's bang in the middle of the clinic hall where the television camera crew are bound to go."

"Excellent," agreed Jess. "Now all we've got to do is work out how to get Rosie out of the box without anybody seeing her."

"Easy," joked Luke.

"Get real! Hiding a pig in a crowd can't be *that* simple," Jess replied.

12

Fortunately Mr and Mrs Church were in orbit the following morning. The press arrived first for their guided tour of the hospital, rapidly followed by the public, all keen to get their first view of the most up-to-date animal hospital in the north-west of England. Beryl was acting as a guide, Mrs Mars, Sam and Beth were serving refreshments, the twins were directing the visitors into parking spaces and Luke and

Jess were supposed to be 'floating', making sure that nobody was where they shouldn't be. It was the ideal role for the pair of them, as one could 'float' while the other kept an eye open for Miss Booth and the trailer. A few minutes after eleven she rolled up the main drive.

"Hello, Miss Booth," called Daisy as she waved her into a parking spot. "Why have you brought your trailer?"

"Oh, I've been picking up feed," Miss Booth explained lightly. "I say, dear, do put me somewhere out of the way. I don't want to be hemmed in by hordes of people when I'm backing out. Would you mind awfully if I parked over there, in that large space near the hospital?"

"That's all right, Miss Booth," Daisy replied. "Help yourself."

At the sound of crunching tyres on the gravel outside, Luke and Jess dashed out of the holding box which they'd been preparing for Rosie. Giggling like naughty school children they huddled together at the back of the trailer trying to work out a strategy.

"I'll go and check where Beryl's guided

tour has got to," Luke said.

"And I'll see where Mum and Dad are," Jess volunteered.

"And I'll stay right here," laughed Miss Booth.

Five minutes later they were both back.

"Mum and Dad are in the operating theatre," Jess announced.

"The public tour's on the other side of the hall, in the recovery boxes," said Luke. "We've got about ten minutes before they pass through here on their way to the intensive care unit outside."

"It's now or never," said Miss Booth heroically.

"Let's go for it!" cried Luke.

Miss Booth dropped the ramp and Rosie looked out at them in surprise. She grunted in delight when she saw her friends but they pressed their fingers to their lips and whispered,"Shshsh!"

Looking a little offended, Rosie obligingly shut up as they led her down the ramp and into the clinic hall which was mercifully empty. Guiding her with pig boards they hurried the majestic pig into the holding box where they instantly shut the doors behind her.

"PHEW!!!" they breathed as they fell against the closed doors, gasping with relief.

"Hi," called Danny, as he innocently wandered by. "What's the matter?"

"Nothing!" they all replied together.

"We're just, er, admiring the clinic hall," said Miss Booth. "It really is quite stunning, don't you think, Danny?"

The boy looked at her as if she'd gone *mad*!

"You've seen it all before, Miss Booth," he reminded her.

"Yes but there's nothing like seeing something again, with fresh eyes," she said quickly.

Suddenly from behind the closed doors came a muffled "HONK!"

"What was that?" asked Danny.

"I didn't hear anything," Luke answered airily.

The noise came again, louder this time. "HONK!"

"There's something in the holding room," Danny cried.

"Don't be daft, of course there's not,"

Luke told him firmly.

Danny marched to the door, his eyes blazing.

"I'm not stupid," he said, reaching for the handle.

At that precise moment, when Luke was on the point of knocking his brother's block off, the television crew drove up.

"Quick, Danny, come with me," cried Jess, running out to meet them.

"That was a close shave," gasped Miss Booth when they'd gone. "Now I'm going to get rid of my trailer before it arouses suspicion. Guard the door," she added imperiously.

Three minutes later she was back with a bucket of pig nuts.

"These should keep Rosie happy for a few minutes," she said, thrusting the bucket into Luke's hands. "See you soon."

Luke cautiously opened the holding room door and peeped in. Smelling the pig nuts Rosie barged forward but Luke dumped the bucket on the floor and while she was eating he quickly arranged a make-shift barrier with the pig boards. He'd only just shut the doors when Beryl strolled through the clinic hall, followed by a large crowd, heading for the intensive care unit. With his heart thumping inside his rib-cage Luke paced the area, desperately trying to look relaxed and casual. When the television crew entered the clinic hall with Mr and Mrs Church he dashed back to the holding box and stood guard. Mum looked at him curiously but didn't have time to ask any questions.

"So where's the best place to set up?" the head cameraman asked her.

"Here, in the clinic hall," Mum told him. "This is where I'll be making my opening speech."

"Excellent," said the cameraman. "Give us ten minutes and we'll be ready to roll."

As the crowd pushed forward to get a better view of the television cameras, a little boy ran towards the holding box and banged on the door. "What's in there?" he asked.

"Oh, nothing much."

"Can I go in?"

"No you can't," Luke whispered firmly. "Go back to your Mum." He was relieved to see Miss Booth slip in, carrying a very large covered basket.

"What've you got in the basket?" he teased. "Our lunch?"

"No, Rosie's," Miss Booth answered as she opened the holding room door and slipped inside.

Luke could hear a happy honk and quite a lot of snuffling coming from behind the closed door. He covered his mouth to hide his smile as he imagined Rosie blissfully tucking into another bucket of pig nuts. Miss Booth reappeared looking rather red and flustered.

"Everything all right?" he asked.

"Fine," she answered breezily.

"Quiet now," called the head cameraman. "We're about to start recording."

A hush fell as Mrs Church stepped forward and started her opening speech. She looked calm and confident in her new cream suit and smart shoes but the family knew she was nervous from the way she kept pressing her lips tightly together.

"The opening of the Sanctuary hospital is a dream come true for me," Mrs Church started. "I first thought of it fifteen years ago, when I was working as a vet in an

131

African safari park. Now my vision is a reality," she added proudly. "It took a lot of hard work, a lot of sacrifice and a lot of money," she said with a smile. "But it's been worth it."

"Hear, hear," yelled all their friends and neighbours in the crowd.

"Moorside Animal Sanctuary is the most advanced veterinary centre in the north of England today and we can all be rightly proud of that achievement!" she said with tears in her eyes.

The crowd cheered and clapped again.

"Well done," shouted Farmer Bracegirdle from the back of the hall.

Just as Mum was about to continue there was a loud honking noise followed by a series of squeaks. The camera crew and audience looked surprised but Mum kept her composure.

"I'd like to thank you all for coming here to share this special moment with me—" she began, but was interrupted by thunderous grunting.

"What's that noise?" asked the boy who'd tried to get into the holding box earlier.

In answer to his question, Luke and

132

Miss Booth winked at each other then swung open the doors of the holding box. There was Rosie, sitting resplendent behind the pig boards, with little Connor beside her. In the stunned silence that followed Miss Booth stepped forwards.

"This is Rosie, my three-year-old prize-winning Gloucester Old Spot," she started proudly, "and Connor, her youngest. She and her litter were the first patients to be treated here at the Sanctuary Large Animal hospital. Under the most tense conditions Mrs Church performed a most difficult operation and Rosie and Connor are here today as living proof of her consummate skill, care and expertise. We are lucky, privileged and honoured to have not one but *two* vets in our neighbourhood who provide the very best to Moorside community and all its many animals."

The crowd went wild. They clapped and cheered and Tara Bracegirdle ran forward with a huge bouquet of Easter lilies for Mrs Church.

"These are from all your friends in Moorside. Thanks for coming here," she said with a broad grin.

With the departure of the camera crew and reporters, the visitors gathered outside in the lovely spring sunshine for a delicious buffet lunch but Luke had only one thought in his mind. He slipped away to visit little Connor who'd been removed from the holding box to a pen in the yard. He found the piglet hungrily suckling from his Mum who was lying on her side, snoozing in the sun.

"Hi, big boy," whispered Luke as he bent down to pick him up. "I've missed you."

"And he's missed you," said Miss Booth coming up behind him.

"You never said you were going to bring Connor," said Luke.

"That was my surprise for *you*," she said. "You know, Luke, he really is your pig."

Luke shuffled awkwardly.

"Life's not quite that simple," he pointed out.

"Stuff and nonsense. I'm giving Connor to you, boy!"

Luke stared at her.

"To me!"

"You must ask your parents' permission,

of course," she added hurriedly. "If they give you the go-ahead he's yours, once he's weaned."

"But he's a valuable, rare pig!" Luke exclaimed. "Don't you want to sell him?"

"Connor needs you, like I need Rosie. Pig people understand these things, you know."

Holding Connor tightly in one hand, Luke held out the other.

"It's a deal," he said, taking hold of Miss Booth's large hand.

"A good deal," she replied, as they vigorously shook hands.

"OINK!" went Connor and the deal was done!

1

New Friends

When the Church family leaves
London to set up an animal
sanctuary in the north of England,
Luke, Jess, Daisy and Danny
have no idea of the adventures
that await them.

They love roaming the moors
with their new friends Sam and
Beth, and caring for the animals.
But it is not long before the
animal sanctuary itself is in
danger when the village turns
against them. How can the
sanctuary survive?

3

Animal Alert

Daisy and Dan are shocked
to discover a young fallow deer
who's been shot. They are
determined to save the deer
and find the culprits.

Meanwhile, Poppy the dog
has puppies, and there is chaos
at the Agricultural Show when
a bull slips his rope and injures
a prize shire horse.

4

Animals at Home

When the lorry delivering a tiger
to the zoo is involved in an
accident, Daisy and Dan rush to
the scene. Can the tiger by saved?

Careless campers also cause
problems for some greedy baby
goats, and the whole family gets
a Christmas surprise when Dora
the donkey goes into labour on
Christmas Eve.